The Power of Gratitude

Bobbie Kalman

Crabtree Publishing Company
www.crabtreebooks.com

Created by Bobbie Kalman

With much love and gratitude to Valerie Kalman, my mother,
for all the ways she helped me become who I am today
and for the wonderful family times we've had together

Author and
Editor-in-Chief
Bobbie Kalman

Editor
Kathy Middleton

Proofreader
Crystal Sikkens

Photo research
Bobbie Kalman

Design
Bobbie Kalman
Katherine Berti
Samantha Crabtree
(text and cover)

Print and production coordinator
Katherine Berti

Images:
Barb Bedell: page 3
Digital Stock: title page
Dreamstime: page 24 (bottom right)
iStockphoto.com: Cover (words HAPPY, CARE); page 28 (words LOVE, CARE, HAPPY)
Shutterstock.com: cover photos (except words made by kids) and all other photographs

Library and Archives Canada Cataloguing in Publication

Title: The power of gratitude / Bobbie Kalman.
Names: Kalman, Bobbie, author.
Description: Series statement: Be your best self: building social-emotional skills | Includes index.
Identifiers: Canadiana (print) 2019013447X | Canadiana (ebook) 20190134488 |
  ISBN 9780778767091 (hardcover) |
  ISBN 9780778767190 (softcover) |
  ISBN 9781427124203 (HTML)
Subjects: LCSH: Gratitude—Juvenile literature. | LCSH: Mindfulness
  (Psychology)—Juvenile literature. | LCSH: Conduct of life—Juvenile literature.
Classification: LCC BJ1533.G8 K35 2019 | DDC j179/.9—dc23

Library of Congress Cataloging-in-Publication Data

Names: Kalman, Bobbie, author.
Title: The power of gratitude / Bobbie Kalman.
Description: New York : Crabtree Publishing Company, [2020] |
  Series: Be your best self: building social-emotional skills | Includes index.
Identifiers: LCCN 2019023864 (print) | LCCN 2019023865 (ebook) |
  ISBN 9780778767091 (hardcover) | ISBN 9780778767190 (paperback) |
  ISBN 9781427124203 (ebook)
Subjects: LCSH: Gratitude in children--Juvenile literature. |
  Gratitude--Juvenile literature.
Classification: LCC BF723.G7 K35 2020 (print) | LCC BF723.G7 (ebook) |
  DDC 179/.9--dc23
LC record available at https://lccn.loc.gov/2019023864
LC ebook record available at https://lccn.loc.gov/2019023865

Crabtree Publishing Company

www.crabtreebooks.com   1-800-387-7650

Printed in the U.S.A./102019/CG20190809

Published in Canada
Crabtree Publishing
616 Welland Ave.
St. Catharines, Ontario
L2M 5V6

Published in the United States
Crabtree Publishing
PMB 59051
350 Fifth Avenue, 59th Floor
New York, New York 10118

Published in the United Kingdom
Crabtree Publishing
Maritime House
Basin Road North, Hove
BN41 1WR

Published in Australia
Crabtree Publishing
Unit 3 – 5 Currumbin Court
Capalaba
QLD 4157

Contents

The gratitude attitude

Gratitude is a way of acting, feeling, and being **aware** that everything in life is a gift. Each time we say "thank you," we are showing respect for what we have. Gratitude changes our lives. It fills us with energy and creativity. It changes our negative feelings to positive ones. Gratitude prevents us from wasting whatever we are grateful for.

The power of gratitude

Gratitude gives us power. Power comes from inside us. We have power over our minds, emotions, and health. Gratitude also gives us greater **self-esteem**, or respect for ourselves. When we live with an attitude of gratitude, we find that more good things happen in our lives. We become more creative and in control of our emotions. We feel more joyful and less afraid or angry. Our happiness makes others happy as well. Happiness spreads quickly. Try it, you'll see it's true!

When you wake up each morning, thank the Sun, Earth, air, and water for keeping you alive. These are your most precious gifts.

Gratitude creates a good feeling in my heart. It makes me feel that I deserve a good life. It helps me love myself and others.

Feeling grateful

Gratitude is an attitude that gives us more control over our lives. It makes us more aware of our **authentic**, or real, selves! Gratitude helps us understand why the gifts we have been given are so special. It helps us become more aware of our connection to everything and everyone. Feeling grateful fills our hearts with love.

Not everyone is healthy or has family, friends, and a home. Do you feel grateful for the good things, like these, that are positive in your life?

5

No one is just like you!

We are all different. We look different. Some of us are girls. Some of us are boys. Skin, eye, and hair color are tiny pieces of information that make us different. Our faces are also not the same. In which other ways are we different? How are we the same?

Grateful for your life

There is no one on Earth who looks, thinks, or acts just like you! The part of you that is different also allows you to create different ideas about your life. You can shape your own life by making choices and decisions about how you want to live. Being grateful for your life is a positive choice that will help you stay healthy and happy.

There is no one just like me.

I'm the best that I can be.

I'm so thankful, oh so grateful, happy to be me!

The authentic you is the one that allows you to love and accept yourself just the way you are. It is the self that loves others and looks at life in a joyful way. You are your authentic self when you are happy with yourself and grateful for the world around you.

Gratitude and happiness

When we are grateful, we feel thankful for the gifts in our lives. That is a good feeling! We can find many things to be grateful for. Happiness is living every moment of life with peace, love, and gratitude. It is a feeling of satisfaction that allows us to deal with everything that happens to us in our lives. It is trusting that we don't have to be afraid of life's challenges. If we can remove fear and worry, we would be left mainly with happiness.

Gratitude is positive

The more thankful we are, the fewer negative thoughts we have. The more we practice and express gratitude, the more self-confident we become. Whether we say "thank you" to someone or receive thanks from others, the feeling it brings is happiness. Gratitude improves our relationships with the people in our lives. Expressing gratitude not only to others but also to ourselves, creates happiness.

Start a gratitude journal!

In your gratitude journal, focus on your good memories and happy moments. Each time you read your journal, you will find that some of the things you have written may be just what you need to focus on, especially on days when you are facing challenges.

Happiness only exists in the present. Make the decision to be happy—NOW!

In your journal, write all the big and small things for which you are thankful.

My Gratitude Journal

Gratitude statements

Gratitude makes us feel better about our lives. Accepting happiness makes us stronger and more grateful for what we have. We learn to praise our efforts and handle the problems in our lives. Gratitude statements, such as the ones below, help you realize how wonderful life is! They make you aware of the good choices you are making in your life. Read the statements and make your own gratitude and happy list.

I am grateful for being a good ukulele player. I play songs that make me and others happy.

- I am grateful for my family.
- Listening to music and dancing make me joyful.
- I love my dog. He keeps me happy!
- I love going to the playground with my friends.
- I am grateful for the beautiful weather we have had this summer.
- Going to school makes me happy. I love my teacher and my friends.
- I am grateful that I live in a safe place.
- I love the food my father cooks.
- I love my grandmother's cookies and cakes.
- I love listening to the birds outside my home.
- I love the vacations I take with my family.

I love sports. I am a great soccer player!

Thank you body!

Your body does many jobs each day. It works hard to keep you growing, moving, and thinking. Your brain is the body part that controls most of your body functions. It keeps you breathing, growing, and moving. It makes sure that your heart pumps blood to all parts of your body. It stores memories—even those you cannot remember.

Gratitude makes us aware of what goes on in our bodies and minds. By having positive thoughts, you can improve your health and get to know who you really are. When you thank your body every day, you are using your mind to tell your body that good health is important to you. Gratitude helps you stay healthy.

You can thank your body by feeding it healthy foods.

Living a healthy life

To be healthy, we need some very important things that all living things need. We need sunshine, clean air to breathe, clean water to drink, and healthy food to eat. We need to be active, and we need plenty of sleep, too. There are things that you can do that will make a big difference in your life.

You can...

- eat foods that are good for your body
- drink plenty of water
- exercise your body at least one hour each day
- have fun playing, laughing, and taking part in activities such as art, music, writing, dancing, and sports
- spend time outdoors every day

Mindfulness and gratitude

Practicing mindfulness means paying attention to our thoughts, feelings, body, and mind in the present moment without making any judgements about them. Practicing mindfulness with gratitude helps us recognize the blessings we have and not react in fear or anger to our problems. Mindfulness helps us face our problems with a calm mind.

Mindful breathing

Breathing is a big part of mindfulness. The steps below will help you learn to breathe mindfully, focusing on your breath.

- Sit in a comfortable position and put both hands on your belly.
- Take a deep breath through your nose. Notice how your in-breath travels down into your lungs, causing your belly to expand and push your hands outward. Is the air cool as you inhale?
- As you exhale, your belly contracts, and the air moves up through your nose or mouth. Does the air feel warm?
- Breathe this way for one minute every hour until you remember to do it when you need it.

Mindfulness helps you be more positive, loving, and grateful for your life. Gratitude and mindfulness will make you happier.

Mindful breathing helps us pay attention to our breath and keeps us in the present moment.

Yoga and you

Yoga exercises help you build balance, strength, and focus. Try the poses shown on this page and see how they make you feel. Be gentle on yourself. Are there other yoga poses that you do often? Which are your favorites?

*The **Camel Pose** gives you courage to face your problems. You have to keep your balance while you bend backwards to grab your heels (or ankles). Can you do this pose? Does it make you feel brave?*

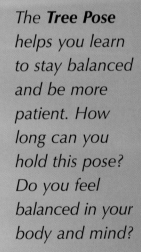

*The **Tree Pose** helps you learn to stay balanced and be more patient. How long can you hold this pose? Do you feel balanced in your body and mind?*

*The **Corpse Pose** is usually the last pose at the end of a yoga session. It thanks your body for all the work it has done.*

*The **Child Pose** helps stretch your hips, thighs, ankles, and arms. It calms you down and helps you be more mindful of your breath.*

Gratitude for my family

Parents or other adults that take care of you provide you with food, shelter, and other things you need. They also teach you lessons about what is important in life. Families can include children, parents, grandparents, aunts, and uncles.

Different families

Some children have one parent and a stepmother or stepfather. They may have sisters and brothers who are not related to them. Other children may have been **adopted** or live in **foster** homes. No matter what kind of family you are a part of, family members care for one another, follow rules, do jobs around the home, respect one another, and have fun.

Grateful in many ways

There are so many ways to show our families that we are grateful. We can say "thank you," but a better way to show our gratitude is by thoughtful actions and kind words. The photos on these pages show ways to share gratitude with your family. Can you come up with your own ways? After all, you know your family best!

Pile up on top of your parents and grandparents and laugh!

Ask your grandparents about your family history. What important events did they live through? They will be happy to share their stories with you!

Surprise your mother with flowers. Tell her that she is a wonderful Mom!

When you sit down for a meal, take turns complimenting your other family members. Your kind words will make the meal taste wonderful!

During sad times is when families need each other the most. Showing love and support for one another is very important.

Share your happy memories of family vacations.

How do you show your pet love? How does your pet show its love for you?

Help your grandparents stay fit by exercising with them.

Grateful for my community

A **community** is a place where many people live and work together. Most communities have buildings as well as outdoor places such as parks. **Neighborhoods** are places where people live. They include houses and apartment buildings. Many communities also have shopping malls, factories, schools, police stations, and fire departments. **Community helpers** are people who work to make communities safe, clean, and healthy. Many community helpers also provide people with information and education.

Firefighters fight fires in buildings and forests. They rescue people who are trapped in fires.

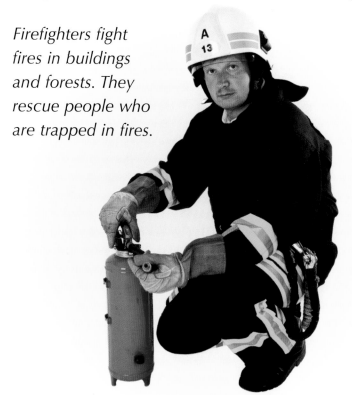

Name the community helpers these children represent.

Which one is a doctor, nurse, veterinarian, firefighter, police officer, or lawyer?

Police officers protect people and keep them safe. This officer is teaching a girl how to call for help in an emergency.

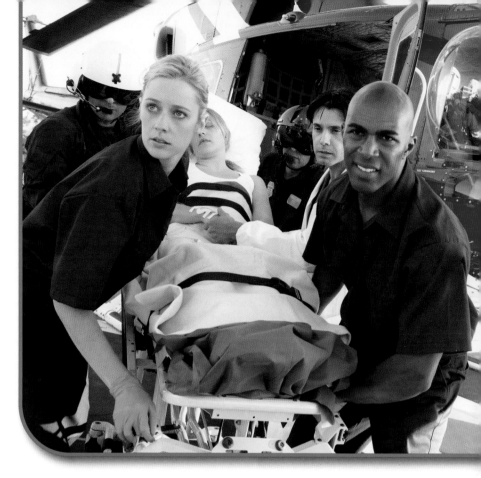

Emergencies are dangerous events that happen suddenly, such as accidents. Emergency workers rescue people in need and care for them until they arrive at the hospital.

Make a list of the community helpers that you would like to thank. Write thank-you notes or letters to those who have helped you or kept you safe.

Doctors, nurses, and many other medical helpers work in hospitals. This girl has had surgery and is in a hospital. She is happy to see her father, who is visiting her. Her doctor tells her that she can go home in a few days.

I love my school!

A school is a community where people share information, classrooms and other rooms, equipment, and outdoor areas, such as playgrounds. Teachers, librarians, principals, nurses, counselors, and custodians are just a few of the people who work in schools. Children build their knowledge at school and participate in sports, music, art, and other acitivies. School is also a place for children to make friends and learn **social skills**. Some of these skills include dealing with emotions, accepting differences, making good decisions, and resolving conflicts.

Our librarian helps us learn about the world and where students in our school have come from.

I am learning to play the guitar in my music class. I am thankful for music. It makes me happy.

I can get around school easily in my wheelchair. My favorite classes are gym and math.

I love my school! I learn a lot and am happy when I'm there. Make a list of all the things you love about your school. What are your favorite subjects and activities? What are you most grateful for?

I love science! It is my favorite subject.

Thank you Earth!

Earth is a miracle planet. It is the only planet in our **solar system** that supports life. Only Earth is the right distance from the Sun—it is neither too hot nor too cold for living things. Only Earth has air, water, plants, animals, and people. Air, water, food, and sunlight connect us to one another, and we depend on one another to survive! We are a part of everything, and everything is a part of us. We are Earth's children!

Earth's gifts to us

When you wake up in the morning, you stretch and yawn and take a deep breath. Do you think of air as a gift? Do you think of water as a gift when you take a bath or shower and brush your teeth? You get dressed and eat your breakfast. Do you think of food as a gift? Air is a gift. Water and food are gifts. The Sun is another gift. It gives us the right amount of light and warmth that we need to survive.

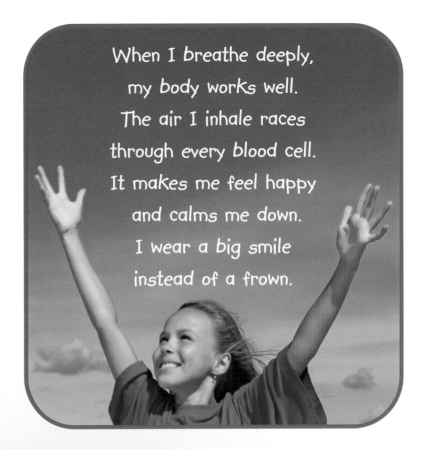

When I breathe deeply, my body works well. The air I inhale races through every blood cell. It makes me feel happy and calms me down. I wear a big smile instead of a frown.

Sun   Venus   Earth   Mars   Jupiter   Saturn   Uranus

Mercury   Neptune

Our solar system consists of the Sun, planets, and moons. The planets are Mercury, Venus, Earth, Mars, Jupiter, Saturn, Uranus, and Neptune. Look at the picture below and name the planets held by the children after you have learned the names of the planets above.

Sun

Thank you air!

Earth is surrounded by layers of air that make up the **atmosphere**. The atmosphere is like a blanket of air around Earth. It protects us from the hot rays of the Sun during the day. It also traps the Sun's heat to keep Earth warm at night. The atmosphere contains the air we breathe. Without air, we could not survive for more than a few minutes.

Breath connects us all

Breathing connects humans to life. It also connects us to other living things. Did you know that every breath of air you take has been breathed by another living thing before? **Oxygen** moves in a cycle. Plants create the oxygen we and other living things breathe in. They use the **carbon dioxide** we breathe out to make their food. They can then make more oxygen.

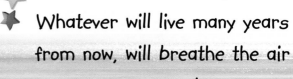
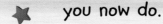

Part of every breath you take
has been breathed
by living things before.
Air is shared by you and me,
as well as so many more.
Air connects us with the past
and with the future, too.
Whatever will live many years
from now, will breathe the air
you now do.

Thank you water!

Did you know that almost three–quarters of Earth is covered by water? Your body is also made up of almost the same **ratio** of water. We are watery creatures living on a watery planet! Most of Earth's water is contained in oceans. Ocean water is **salt water**, or water that contains a lot of salt, but the water in rivers and lakes is **fresh water**. Fresh water does not contain a lot of salt. We need to drink fresh water to stay alive.

We are connected to other living things by water. The water **vapor** we exhale becomes part of clouds. The water in clouds may fall as rain or snow. Plants, animals, and people then drink that water. You need to drink from 6 to 8 glasses of water each day! When you are thankful for water, you will value it as a gift that keeps you alive. Read the poem below and write your own poem about why you are grateful for water.

Most of Earth is covered in water.
Most of our bodies are water, too.
Our bones and brains
and the blood in our veins
need water to do the work
that they do.
Without water,
we could not survive!
Without water,
we would not be alive.
Our hearts could not beat.
We'd have nothing to eat.
Our brains could not think
without water to drink!

23

Grateful for our food

People and animals need sunlight, air, and water in order to survive, but they also need food. Food gives us energy to move and do the things we want to do. Plants can make their own food using water, the carbon dioxide in air, and the energy of the Sun.

Thank you plants!

Unlike plants, animals and people cannot make their own food in their bodies. By eating plants, or animals that have eaten plants, we take in the energy that the plants received from the Sun. Without plants, there would be no food! Plants give us delicious fruits and vegetables. They also feed the animals from which we get many of our other foods. Most people eat both fruit and vegetables, as well as food that comes from animals, such as meat, milk, and eggs.

Plants take in sunlight through their leaves.

Their leaves make oxygen for us to breathe.

Plants also take in air (carbon dioxide) through their leaves.

Plants take in water through their roots.

*These chickens are eating **grains**, or seeds. People eat the eggs from chickens as well as their meat.*

Name the parts of this sandwich that came from plants. Name the foods that came from animals. Make a list of your favorite foods, and name the source of each food.

24

What kind of eater is this girl? What kind of eater are you? Read the poem and find out.

What are your foods?

Animals are living things.
Living things are alive.
Food gives animals energy,
to grow, move, and survive.
Some animals eat mainly plants.
They are called **herbivores**.
Other animals eat mainly meat.
They are called **carnivores**.
Omnivores are animals
that eat both plants and meat.
They survive very well
on the different foods they eat.
You are an omnivore if you eat
veggies, fruit, and meat!

*This **vegetarian** family has a garden. They make **preserves** from the fruits and vegetables they grow. They use the preserves in winter.*

Sharing with others

Gratitude makes us realize how fortunate we are to have food. Part of gratitude is sharing our gifts with others who need our help. Many people on Earth, or even in your community, do not have enough food to eat. You and your classmates can work together as a team and volunteer to help others who need food.

Many people have lost their homes due to floods and tornadoes. Shelters and soup kitchens help feed those people.

Thanksgiving every day

Thanksgiving is a holiday celebrated in North America and other countries around the world. It is a holiday that brings families together from near and far to give thanks for family, friends, food, and good health. Families often recall happy times in the past and share future plans. Favorite Thanksgiving foods are turkey and pumpkin pie.

Thanks for sharing!

Sharing your stories

While you are eating dinner with your family, share the things that have happened to you over the past year for which you are thankful. You can also do this with your friends. Sit in a circle. After the first person tells his or her story, the second friend can repeat it before telling his or her story. In this way, the happiness of each person will be enjoyed by everyone.

Showing your thanks

This page gives examples of other ways you can show your thanks each day. No matter how you thank someone, you will feel happy, and so will the person that you thank. Your own way of saying thanks will be the most meaningful.

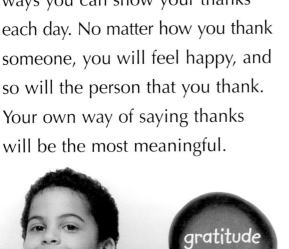

Write thank–you messages on hearts for family and friends.

Fill a jar with messages of gratitude. When the jar is full, take out a note each day to remember why you wrote the message and how it made you feel.

Write what you are grateful for each day in your gratitude journal.

Make up a gratitude song and sing it often to yourself and the people you want to thank.

Draw or write something on a board that...
- makes you feel happy
- makes you smile or laugh
- you think is fun
- has helped you
- made you a better you

Paint a picture of nature and share it with others to remember Earth's gifts to us.

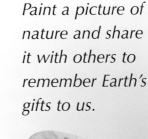

THANK-YOU ALPHABET

The alphabet game is a fun gratitude activity. Use letters to create words that best describe why you are thankful. You and some friends can also use your bodies to make up words, like the kids on this page. See how they do it, and have fun making your own body words.

HAPPY CHILDREN
LOVE PLEASE YES
LETTERS CARE

More gratitude words

What are you most grateful for? Look at the words below. What feelings rise in your heart when you say each word? Answer the questions beneath the words and then share your gratitude stories. What other words would you add?

Which of your dreams have come true? What are your dreams for the future?

What makes you smile? How grateful are you for each smile?

What is the most important gift you have ever received?

What kinds of games, sports, or music do you like to play? Do you play any musical instruments?

Who are the people you love the most? What activities do you do with them that make you happy?

Does dancing make you happy? What are your favorite dance moves?

Name five things that make you happy and tell a story about each.

What is your favorite subject? What will you study when you are older?

What makes you feel powerful? Do you have power over your feelings?

Having fun makes us feel happy. Name the ten most fun things you do often.

Pay it forward!

When we appreciate our lives, we become aware of how fortunate we truly are. We focus on the positive and not the negative. By being thankful for everything in our lives, we are giving our minds a new message that certain things are important to us. You may be just one person in this world, but to people you help, you are the world!

Pay it Forward Day

Pay It Forward Day is a worldwide celebration of kindness that takes place every year on April 28th. It is about people giving to other people without expecting anything in return. This special day encourages all of us to show each other that we care and that there is love, hope, and gratitude all around us. We don't have to be kind and giving just on this day, however. What if each individual looked for the opportunity to help others each day? Imagine the difference that would make!

*Brainstorm ideas with your classmates on how you can help someone or be kind to someone who needs your help. Make posters to get others involved. Everyone can make a difference, and those that you help will also want to help others. Kindness has a **butterfly effect**. When one person is kind, that kindness can spread and change the lives of many people.*

Help a friend learn how to read.

Help raise money for children who lost their homes due to extreme weather. Make a card for a friend. Offer to babysit so your parents can have more free time.

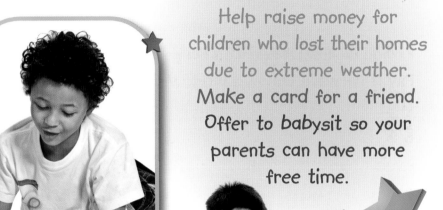

Bring a gift to a child in a homeless shelter. Spend more time with your grandparents.

Donate clothes, books, and toys.

Glossary

Note: Some boldfaced words are defined where they appear in the book.

adopt Legally raise a child as one's own

atmosphere Gases surrounding Earth

authentic Real; genuine

aware Having knowledge of a fact or situation

butterfly effect The idea that a small change in one place can have a big effect elsewhere

carbon dioxide A gas in air that is exhaled by people and used by plants to make food

community A group of people who live or work together

community helper A person who helps others in their community

foster To take care of a child who is not one's own, often for a short time

grains The seeds of plants grown for food

neighborhood A community where people live

oxygen A gas found in air that is needed by people to survive

preserve Food made from fruits or vegetables that is made to last by adding sugar or vinegar

ratio A way to compare two numbers of the same kind

self-esteem Confidence in one's self

social skills The skills we use to communicate and interact with others

solar system The planets and moons that travel around the Sun

vapor Water that has become a part of air after it was heated

vegetarian A person who does not eat meat

Index